Lyon

Lyon

A First-Start Easy Reader

This easy reader contains only 48 different words,
repeated often to help the young reader develop
word recognition and interest in reading.

Basic word list for *Let's Get a Pet*

a	have	some
and	hop	squeak
are	it	take
back	kind	talk
bark	let's	that
big	little	there
can	love	they
care	must	to
clean	of	very
do	our	walk
especially	pet	we
fast	pets	what
feed	play	when
fun	should	will
get	sing	with
good	slow	you

Let's Get a Pet

Written by Rose Greydanus

Illustrated by Lynn Sweat

Troll Associates

Library of Congress Cataloging in Publication Data

Greydanus, Rose.
  Let's get a pet.

  (A First-start easy reader)
  Summary: A boy and girl getting ready to pick out a
pet talk about the many different kinds and their
advantages before finally making their decision.
  [1. Pets—Fiction] I. Sweat, Lynn, ill. II. Title.
III. Series.
PZ7.G876Lc   1988   [E]   87-10938
ISBN 0-8167-0986-6 (lib. bdg.)
ISBN 0-8167-0987-4 (pbk.)

Do you have a pet?

Pets are fun to have.

Let's get a pet!

You can play with pets.

And they will play with you.

You can talk to pets.

And they will talk to you.

You can walk with pets.

And they will walk with you.

What kind of pet will we get?

Some pets are very little.

And some are very big.

Some pets are very fast.

And some are very slow.

There are pets that bark . . .

pets that squeak . . .

pets that hop . . .

and pets that sing!

What kind of pet should we get?

You must take good care of a pet.

You must feed it.

You must clean it.

You must love it.

We will get *that* pet.

We will love our pet!

Do you have a pet?

Pets are fun to have.

Especially when they love you back!